"Come quick! It's the dragon!"

"Let's build a trading post," Tom said. "Natty, you keep an eye out. Might be some bandits or coyotes."

Tom and Emily began to stack bales of hay. Suddenly Natty yelled, "Tom! Come quick! It's the dragon!"

"We're cowboys, Natty, remember?" said Tom. "Cowboys don't—"

"No, Tom, look! Smoke! Right where the treehouse is! See?"

"Ain't no smoke, Natty." Tom picked up another bale. "No dragon, either."

"There is too!" yelled Natty, kicking some loose hay into the air.

Tom stomped to the window and squinted at the trees. For a moment he thought he might have seen something, but he wasn't sure. At any rate, there was nothing there now, nothing at all.

Then Tom had an idea. "Natty," he said in the most matter-of-fact tone he could manage, "maybe you're right. Maybe there is a dragon under the treehouse."

Both Natty and Emily stared at him in astonishment.

"If Emily and I get rid of the dragon once and for all," Tom continued, "will that satisfy you?"

Natty looked out the window, then back at Tom. He nodded, his eyes wide.

Treehouse Tales

ANNE ISAACS

illustrations by

LLOYD BLOOM

PUFFIN BOOKS

PUFFIN BOOKS
Published by the Penguin Group
Penguin Putnam Books for Young Readers,
345 Hudson Street, New York, New York 10014, U.S.A.
Penguin Books Ltd, 27 Wrights Lane, London W8 5TZ, England
Penguin Books Australia Ltd, Ringwood, Victoria, Australia
Penguin Books Canada Ltd, 10 Alcorn Avenue, Toronto, Ontario, Canada M4V 3B2
Penguin Books (N.Z.) Ltd, 182-190 Wairau Road, Auckland 10, New Zealand

Penguin Books Ltd, Registered Offices: Harmondsworth, Middlesex, England

First published in the United States of America by Dutton Children's Books,
a division of Penguin Books USA Inc., 1997
Published by Puffin Books,
a member of Penguin Putnam Books for Young Readers, 1999

1 3 5 7 9 10 8 6 4 2

THE LIBRARY OF CONGRESS HAS CATALOGED THE DUTTON EDITION AS FOLLOWS:
Isaacs, Anne.
Treehouse tales / by Anne Isaacs ; illustrated by Lloyd Bloom.—1st ed. p. cm.
Summary: Three chapters relate the experiences and adventures of three 1880s
Pennsylvania farm children in their family tree house, which serves as a refuge,
a source of adventure, a lookout post, and a frightening dragon's lair.
ISBN 0-525-45611-2
[1. Tree houses—Fiction. 2. Brothers and sisters—Fiction.
3. Farm life—Pennsylvania—Fiction. 4. Pennsylvania—Fiction.]
I. Bloom, Lloyd, ill. II. Title.
PZ7.I762Tr 1997 [Fic]—dc20 96-24549 CIP AC

Puffin Books ISBN 0-14-038738-2

Printed in the United States of America

For Jordan, Amy, and Sarah,
with love

A.I.

To Zalman Kleinman,
his memory should be a blessing

L.B.

Contents

THE DRAGON'S TOOTH

1

TREEHOUSE FEVER

27

THAT STORY ABOUT THE CHERRY TREE

65

The Dragon's Tooth

August
1 8 8 1

Shortly after morning chores, three Union army generals struggled up the battleground of Malvern Hill. General Ulysses S. Grant, covered with sweat and hay, gained the top first and raised the Union flag triumphantly. A fitful summer breeze flapped its corners. The other generals straggled behind, weighed down by cannon and ammunition.

"Wait up! The cannon's stuck!" called General George McClellan. He tugged at a stout oak log that was caught in the haystack.

"I'll trade you, Natty. You can carry the ammunition," General William T. Sherman said sweetly. The general's apron sagged under the weight of the cannonballs, which had been selected for their roundness that very morning from the stream.

"He's not Natty; he's General McClellan!" ordered General Grant impatiently from the top of the haystack. "If you can't carry a cannon, you can't be in our war," he added, looking down at his brother. Natty's short legs sank deeper into the hay as he fought with the log. Soon he was up to his waist.

Tom, forgetting to be General Grant, allowed the flag to drop from his hand. How could anyone pursue adventure and glory with a sister and brother like these? he thought. In the stories Pa had told him about the war, lines of troops half a mile long stormed into battle as if they were one man, their bayonets gleaming like a forest of steel trees. Of course, Pa had been too young to fight, but he'd dreamed of being a scout like his older brother, Eli.

"The war'll be over before General McClellan gets up here," Tom told Emily with exasperation.

"Consider his age, General Grant," she said. "He'll catch up." As she spoke, her apron gave way with a loud rip. Cannonballs clattered through the torn muslin and disappeared into the haystack.

Tom groaned and looked toward the far hills, as if hoping to see a regiment sweep out of the trees. Age was just the problem, he thought. Here he was ten, able to chop wood or hitch a wagon nearly as fast as Pa. Emily was a distant eight, and a girl besides. As for Natty, he'd probably be five forever. It seemed to him that they would never catch up, only hold him back.

"Why don't you two go search for enemy spies in the woods?" Tom said.

"Maybe we should play in the treehouse," suggested Emily. "It's a perfect fort."

"Don't *I* know that?" said Tom. He trudged down the haystack, lifted his brother and the log, then set them gently on the ground. "I was planning to take some rebels back to the fort with us, but I guess we may as well go there without them." He reached for Natty's hand.

"The *tree*house?" Natty pulled his hand away.

"Oh, Natty, not again," pleaded Tom.

"Right on top of the dragon's den? I ain't going near there. Dragon'll breathe fire on me!"

"Now why would I build a treehouse on top of a drag-on's den?" said Tom. "You saw me building it three weeks ago, remember? It's just a hollow stump under there."

"Then how come it's burned all black inside?" asked Natty.

"How should I know? Lightning, maybe. Look, I never heard of no dragons living in Pennsylvania, or anyplace else these days. It's 1881, Natty. Emily's been reading you too many of those fairy stories," he added with a touch of contempt.

Natty shook his head. "I seen smoke coming out of those trees a few days ago, right where the treehouse is. I seen it before, too. I ain't playing there."

"Hang it all, Natty, can't you tell the difference between a little fog and a dragon?" Tom moaned. If only he didn't have to look after Emily and Natty for the whole day while their parents went to Brewster's Mill to trade.

"Listen, Tom," said Emily. "Let's go up to the hayloft. We can make walls of hay for a fort if we clear a space by the window."

"But the treehouse is better. Better than anyplace." Tom's voice was tight with frustration. "You can spy in almost every direction without anyone knowing you're there."

"The hayloft! The hayloft!" said Natty, clapping his hands. "I'm gonna spy on redcoats."

"Wrong war. You mean greycoats," whispered Emily. She buttoned Natty's boots down the sides. "We're playing Civil War. The redcoats fought in the Revolution."

"I'll tell you what, Natty," said Tom. "You come to the treehouse with me and Emmy and just look it over. I promise there'll be no dragons. Then, if you don't want to stay, we'll go to the loft."

Natty hesitated, dancing from one foot to the other. Tom looked at Emily imploringly.

"I'll keep right by you," she said, taking Natty's hand.

"Just a look," said Natty. "I ain't saying I'll stay."

Tom led the way across the farmyard. "I chose the old chestnut stump on purpose," he said. "It's the perfect place—close by, but hidden. The stump was easy to build on, too, soon as Pa helped me set the floor level.

"It took me all of July to saw those branches for the walls," he added quickly. "The walls are the best part, Natty. You'd think you couldn't see out, but you can—the spaces between the branches are like spy holes."

"We shouldn't call it a treehouse," said Emily, "because it's not up in the branches of a tree, like *Swiss Family Robinson*."

"Well, you can't call it a stumphouse," said Tom testily. "Anyway, that hollow stump is mighty handy. Emily and me keep all kinds of things in there, books, marbles—"

"You put your *hand* in there?" asked Natty, wide-eyed.

Tom pretended not to hear. They passed the pigsty and chicken coop and entered the chestnut grove, which stood across the yard from their house. The glare and heat of the farmyard melted away as soon as they stepped into the trees. It was like taking off a heavy coat, Tom thought.

He walked in front, pushing his way through the dense tangle of undergrowth. The huge leaves of the oaks and chestnuts shivered in a light breeze. Long filmy rays of sunlight slanted through the branches. A chorus of insects droned. The ground was spongy with a layer of old leaves.

Suddenly a bobwhite whistled and rose from the brush beside Tom, its feathers flashing russet. It blustered off into the trees.

"I want to go back," Natty said, pulling on Emily's hand.

Tom stared at him.

"I'm hungry," Natty persisted.

"How about you go on up," Tom offered, "and I'll bring you and Emily some rations?"

"I want to go to the loft," said Natty.

"Oh, all right," said Tom wearily. "I'll go forage for rations and meet you in the barn." He spun and headed toward the house.

"You call *them* soldiers?" he muttered as he marched back, slapping hay off his pants. "I tell you half of them are girls, and the other half are cowards." He cast a long-suffering look toward the chestnut grove.

Tom wore his father's high, front-lacing boots to set him apart from his subordinate officers. Even though he'd grown three inches in the last year, Pa's boots were still far too large. His legs ached from the effort of walking in them as he trudged up the steps to the porch.

A weathered felt hat hung on a nail by the door. Zeke, their nearest neighbor and occasional hired hand, had come to keep an eye on things while his parents were in town.

Tom bristled at the thought that one of those things was himself. Hadn't Pa said, as Tom harnessed the horses that morning, that he was getting old enough to drive the wagon? Still, he couldn't help feeling glad that Zeke was there. Zeke had been a cowboy, explorer, and soldier; he had an endless stock of stories. And he was a wonderful cook, Tom reminded himself as he caught the aromas wafting from the kitchen. Perhaps the day held possibilities after all.

"Can you tell me where your ma hid the pepper?" Zeke growled when he saw Tom.

Tom looked from the plate of eggs and sausage steaming on the table to the clean pots hanging on their pegs. He wondered how Zeke always managed to cook a meal without making any mess.

"It was on the table at breakfast," said Tom, his mouth watering. He thought of his mother cooking by lantern light while his father and Zeke coaxed hogs into the back of the wagon. Tom had been up so early that he had done half his chores before sunrise.

"Breakfast? My stomach can't remember that far back," Zeke grumbled. "Here it is!" he added, pulling a pepper mill from a shelf.

Zeke sat down at the table. "What brings you in here?" He looked at Tom suspiciously. "This here's barely tolerable for one, and I suppose you'll want most of it," he muttered, although to Tom it looked like enough for a regiment.

Then Zeke cheerfully heaped food on a plate, sent pepper raining on the eggs, and slid the plate across the table toward Tom. Tom thought that Zeke had the widest smile he'd ever seen. And his ears stuck out farther than anyone's, too. It was as if his smile had nudged his ears into prominence.

Pa had once said that, if the weather changed as often as Zeke's moods, no one could do any farming. "Thank you, Zeke," Tom said, and sat down to eat.

"Where are your brother and sister?" Zeke asked.

"At the barn," Tom told him. "I came to get Natty some apples. We're playing Civil War—leastways, I was."

A shade crossed Zeke's face; he glanced keenly at Tom before he reached across the table for the coffeepot. Tom's cheeks burned. He remembered, too late, that Zeke didn't like to talk about the war, seldom mentioned his years as an infantryman in the 69th New York.

After they had eaten in silence for several minutes, Zeke rose from the table and cleared away his dishes. He hoisted a huge bowl and dumped a mountain of bread dough onto the table. Tom watched Zeke's powerful hands kneading the bread, lifting the heavy dough and whacking it down.

"Your pa took you by Gettysburg when you moved here from Philadelphia, didn't he?" Zeke asked. He broke off a large piece of dough and handed it to Tom, then began to shape the rest into round loaves.

Tom nodded. "We walked through most of the battlefields." He pounded the dough with his fists. "Pa showed me where Colonel Chamberlain, his two brothers, and three hundred men from the Twentieth Maine held off nearly the whole rebel army on Little Round Top. If it wasn't for them, the rebs could've taken Washington in a lick. I picked up a hatful of bullets in Devil's Den," he added. He rolled the dough into three ropes and began to braid them.

"Don't wish too hard to be a soldier, Tom," said Zeke in a tone that made Tom look up. "War isn't all honor and heroism." He lifted the bread bowl and started across the room, limping slightly.

Tom watched him walk. Pa had told him that Zeke had been hit by a piece of shell in the battle of Fredericksburg. The fragment had been removed, but the muscle hadn't healed properly, and his leg had never been the same.

Tom imagined Zeke lying on a muddy battlefield, pelted by hail and freezing rain. He wondered if Zeke had remained conscious after being hit. What if—Tom felt sick at the thought—a doctor had wanted to amputate the leg and Zeke had had to fight to save it?

"I best get outside while these loaves are rising," said Zeke. "Promised your pa I'd fix that fence where the cows broke through." Zeke winked. "Haven't mended fences since the Texas Republic. Hope I remember how."

"Wish you had some time free," Tom said. "I wish . . ." His voice faded. He looked out the window toward the barn.

Zeke clapped a hand on Tom's shoulder. "A little excitement would do you some good. Say, a train robbery—or a gold rush."

"Seems like everything interesting happens someplace else."

Zeke nodded. "My folks lived back in the hills. My first friend was a squirrel."

Tom couldn't help laughing.

"Know what I do when I feel like that?" said Zeke. He reached to the bottom of the deep pocket in his leather vest and pulled out a small, irregular stone,

sharply pointed at one end. It was shiny, as if rubbed. "What would you say this is?"

Tom ran his finger over it. "Except for those swirly lines, it looks like a plain old stone," he said. "Is it valuable?"

"Valuable!" said Zeke, lowering his voice to a gruff whisper. "This is a bear's claw, an arrowhead, a diamond off the queen of England's crown. It's a tiger's fang, the clapper from the Liberty Bell, the magic tip of a wizard's wand. Oh, it can take you off into some hair-straightening adventures."

He glanced sidelong at Tom. "Did I ever tell you about the time I was arrested for stealing my own herd of cattle?"

Tom shook his head and grinned expectantly.

Zeke sat down beside him. "Well, one day while I was out looking for strays, a rustler came along and changed the brands on all my cows. Next morning he brought in the sheriff and had me arrested, claiming they were his cattle and I'd stolen them!

"Before long I was in jail, staring out the bars at a gallows. All I had with me was this stone." Zeke stood up and stretched. "It's a long story, Tom. Natty's waiting, and so's the fence."

"Hang the fence, and Natty, too!" Tom said, jumping up. "You can't stop now!"

"I'll tell you what, Tom. If you keep Em and Natty happy in the barn a spell, I'll do more'n just finish the story."

Tom looked at a pipe stem sticking out of Zeke's vest pocket. "Will you teach me to blow smoke rings?"

"You know your ma don't fancy me smoking myself, never mind teaching you."

"She says your pipe smokes worse'n a locomotive engine."

He chuckled. "No, Tom, I had in mind to teach you how to use a lariat."

"A lariat? Here?" As far as Tom knew, lariats were only for cowboys, and cowboys only lived west of the Mississippi.

"Anyone who works with cows ought to know how to use a rope," Zeke replied. "You'll practice on tree stumps, same as I did. And you'll learn on the ground before you try anything on horseback."

"I'll be ready," said Tom eagerly. He grabbed some apples from a bowl, stuffed them in his pockets, and hurried down the steps.

"Stay in the barn till I come for you, hear?" Zeke called after him. "In case of rain."

Tom glanced at the sky as he walked across the yard. "Blue as cornflowers. No call to worry about rain," he said with a shrug.

Emily and Natty were waiting outside the barn with a present.

"I found it in the woods," said Natty, handing a long stick to Tom. "I peeled the bark for you."

"It's a new sword, General Grant," Emily explained.

"Much obliged." Tom slid his hands along the smooth surface of the stick, which was as tall as Natty and curved like a new moon. He hesitated a moment. "I was thinking we'd play cowboys now."

Natty's face fell. "But I peeled the bark."

"It'll make a fine branding iron," Tom offered.

"You said we could spy," said Natty.

"Then let's get a lookout posted, before rustlers steal our cattle." Tom hurried up the ladder to the hayloft and clambered over bales of hay toward a window that offered a view of their farmyard, fields, and woods.

"We'll stand watch together," he told Natty. "I brought provisions," he added, handing him an apple.

They knelt by the window, crunching their apples. The only other sounds were the cooing of mourning doves, the subdued whine of insects.

The weather vane on the roof of their house turned lightly in the breeze. Watching it, Tom remembered when Pa and Zeke built the roof. The vane, shaped like a three-masted ship, had once stood on their house in Philadelphia. Tom was the only one of the children to recall anything of their life in the great city four years ago. He remembered it as a tantalizing parade of merchants, wagons, and horse-drawn trolleys.

Beyond the house and stretching as far as he could see stood a field of buckwheat, the stalks golden and as tall as Tom. Soon it would be time for Uncle Eli and his two sons to come help with the harvest.

Tom wiped his face with his sleeve. It was hot enough up there to bake bread, he thought. His eye fell on a red-handled pump beside the house. He'd helped Pa paint the handle so it would be easy to find in the deep snow of winter. He eyed it longingly. He figured he could drink a whole bucket of water just now.

"Watching you spy isn't very much fun," Emily observed.

"Let's build a trading post," Tom told her. "Natty, you keep an eye out. Might be some bandits or coyotes."

Tom and Emily began to stack bales of hay. Suddenly Natty yelled, "Tom! Come quick! It's the dragon!"

"We're cowboys, Natty, remember?" said Tom. He struggled to haul a bale into place. "Cowboys don't—"

"No, Tom, look! Smoke! Right where the treehouse is! See?"

"Ain't no smoke, Natty." Tom picked up another bale. "No dragon, either."

"There is too!" yelled Natty, kicking some loose hay into the air. "Just like last time!" He turned back to the window, fuming.

"I'm going to get some provisions for trading." Tom started down the ladder. "Come on, Emmy." But they had barely reached the bottom when Natty began to shout.

"Smoke! Smoke!" he cried. He ran to the top of the ladder and repeated his cry until Tom and Emily came up.

Tom stomped to the window and squinted at the trees. For a moment he thought he might have seen something, but he wasn't sure. Waves of heat trembled over the farmyard. His eyes might be playing tricks on him. At any rate, there was nothing there now, nothing at all.

What was he going to do with Natty? He'd heard about people seeing things while delirious with a high fever. He felt Natty's forehead. He was hot, of course—it must be one hundred degrees in the hayloft—but not feverish.

Then Tom had an idea. "Natty," he said in the most matter-of-fact tone he could manage, "maybe you're right. Maybe there is a dragon under the treehouse."

Both Natty and Emily stared at him in astonishment.

"If Emily and I get rid of the dragon once and for all," Tom continued, "will that satisfy you?"

Natty looked out the window, then back at Tom. He nodded, his eyes wide.

"Stick close to me," Tom told him. "I'll keep you safe."

Tom slid down the ladder, grabbed a bucket from a cow's stall, and crossed the yard. When he pumped the red handle, there was a loud gurgling noise. Water gushed into the bucket.

"What are you going to do?" whispered Natty. He looked as if he were about to cry.

"Well, I never killed a dragon before," said Tom. "But they're mostly fire. If I pour water on him, he should just melt away, don't you think? Like old coals."

"Better watch out. He might be hungry." Natty glanced nervously toward the trees.

"Don't worry," Tom said, grinning. "I heard that dragons don't like the taste of boys."

Natty did not seem to take comfort from this fact.

"I don't think they eat at *all* when it's hot," Tom added.

Natty's lip began to tremble.

"They're what you might call *particular* eaters," Tom concluded, feeling that he had pretty much made a mess of it.

The bucket was full. "Here I go, Natty," he said. "I promise you'll never see a dragon in this forest again."

Tom picked up the bucket and jostled through the grove, pushing branches out of his way with his free arm. He'd better soak the inside of the stump, he decided, to show Natty that the dragon had been melted down to nothing. Maybe he'd crash around in the brush near the treehouse to make it sound like a fight. He grinned, imagining it.

Tom reached the treehouse without spilling much.

He'd gotten so strong from pitching hay that summer that his arm hardly ached. As he shifted his grip on the bucket, he smelled a pungent aroma, out of place but oddly familiar. He stopped and looked up.

It was then that he saw the smoke. A swirling white plume rose above the treehouse wall.

Without thinking, he sprang forward and heaved water up at the treehouse. He had barely enough time to imagine it in flames before he hurled the remaining water.

Instantly a sound like the howl of a wounded beast split the air. Tom froze in horror and let the empty bucket bang to the ground. Then he spun around and tore through the trees to the pump, where Emily and Natty crouched, silent and wide-eyed.

"Did you get it?" asked Natty.

"I got *something*," said Tom. He could hear his heart pounding. It *couldn't* be a dragon, could it? He stared at the chestnut grove, shaken by sudden misgivings.

It might be a bear, he thought. Or a hawk. Sometimes the pigs made a sound like that. But how would a pig get up there?

The sound came again, shattering the afternoon still-ness: *"AIEE . . ."*

"Don't sound like no fussy eater to me," said Natty.

At that moment something crashed toward them through the chestnut saplings, setting the leaves trembling. It swore loudly as it came. First a boot, then a wet pant leg, and finally a furious, spluttering Zeke emerged from the trees and staggered in a circle in front of the astonished children.

What was Zeke doing in the treehouse? thought Tom.

Zeke shook water off his beard. "Mighty blue sky for a downpour!" he bellowed, glaring at the children. The stem of a pipe showed above his clenched fist.

Tom stared at the pipe. So Zeke was the dragon! Natty was right after all. Tom began to laugh. No wonder Zeke wanted us to stay in the barn, he thought. And it did rain, but only on Zeke!

"Did *you* kill the dragon?" Natty asked Zeke.

Zeke stopped and stared at Natty. He plunged the pipe in the pocket of his vest. Water dripped from his matted hair onto his face.

"Sure he did!" said Tom, grinning. "Dragon almost got him first. You should've seen those claws! But Zeke fought like fury, and the water finished the job. All that was left was a big pile of green-and-purple scales; they melted away, too, after a bit. The dragon's clean gone,

Natty. You won't see any more smoke coming from the treehouse."

Zeke looked startled. Then a sly smile spread across his face. "Ye-es," he drawled. "No telling what would have happened if Tom hadn't come along with that bucket." He took something from his vest pocket and beckoned to Natty. "Come here, Nat, and see what that dragon left behind."

Zeke held out the stone he had shown Tom in the house. "Tell him what it is, Tom."

"Looks like one of the dragon's teeth," said Tom.

"Its teeth looked like *that*? No wonder they never smile," said Natty. Then he added, "You always said there aren't any—"

"No telling what'll turn up, if you're scouting for adventures," Tom broke in. "Even on our farm." He regarded his brother with new feeling. For one moment Natty had brought a dragon to life on their homestead.

"What if another one moves in?" asked Natty.

"Fact is, I think this was the last dragon," Zeke told him. "From now on there'll only be spiders in that stump."

"I like *them*," said Natty. "I'm hungry!" he added.

"You're always hungry," said Emily.

"Getting rid of dragons can work up a powerful appetite,"

Zeke said with a smile. He put the dragon's tooth back in his vest. "Emmy, you run to the root cellar and bring back the six biggest potatoes you can find. Tom, you gather up some green leaves. Nat and me will build a fire on the ground in the yard." He began to collect sticks.

"Are we having potatoes and leaves for dinner?" asked Natty.

"Just plain roast potatoes. Kansas style. Leaves keep the skins from burning."

"Why aren't we cooking indoors?" said Emily, returning with potatoes in her arms.

"Well, for one thing, it ain't the cowboy way," said Tom. "Cowboys go for months without seeing a house, let alone living in one. Besides, food tastes better cooked outdoors." He picked up a leaf, then stooped to examine a small stone. It was reddish brown, cratered with tiny holes and scored by black lines. It looked powerful, ancient. Tom stood and turned the stone over in his hand.

"Straight out of the Milky Way," he murmured. "Blazing through the Kansas sky, aiming directly for my cattle. Stampede? No, sir! Caught it with my lariat before it reached the earth."

Tom smiled and put the stone deep in a pocket of his trousers.

Treehouse Fever

August
1 8 8 3

Emily sat against the treehouse wall and gazed into the restless leaves. "A full moon lights the tower," she whispered. "Now is my chance to signal the prince." She unwound one of her waist-long braids and knelt to shake her hair loose. "Give me Rosamond, your fastest horse," she called into the trees. "I shall gallop to freedom! Once I begin to ride, nothing will stop me. I'll fly through the woods! My hair will stream behind me like a royal banner. No one in the kingdom will catch me. Bring Rosamond to me at midnight, garbed in silver, a token of your everlasting—"

"PIGS!" Tom shouted in the direction of the tree-house. He trudged across the barnyard to the house, a full milk bucket in each hand. *"Feed-the-*PIGS!" he called again.

Emily heard Tom shouting. She caught glimpses of her brothers through the shifting leaves of the chestnut grove and saw them look her way. Her stomach tightened.

"I'll bet they can hear our pigs all the way to Brewster's Mill," Tom said to Natty. "Can't *she* hear 'em? What's got into her?"

Natty followed Tom, polishing a clay whistle with a smooth stone. "Treehouse fever," he said.

"What?" Tom set the heavy buckets on the porch.

Natty shrugged. "Whenever she's up there, she talks like she's off in the head. Princes, garbled horses, I don't know what-all. I figure, it's that treehouse."

"Ain't the treehouse. It's account of she's a girl." Tom looked at Natty with a knowing air. "They all get that way."

Natty glanced toward the treehouse. "Girl!" he said, as if he had been told his sister were a snail. He ran up the steps, testing his whistle, and held the door for Tom. "How's it sound?" he asked.

"Like an owl with a sore throat." Tom grinned and carried the buckets inside.

Emily climbed down the treehouse ladder and stomped toward the farmyard. It was bad enough that Tom had stopped playing with her and confiding in her; he didn't have to be so bossy, too. Lately he put on airs just because he was allowed to ride Pa's horse, Rosie. He sat on Rosie like a general parading before his troops, she thought. It was true he'd ridden to Brewster's Mill three times, but to hear him talk you'd think he'd discovered a new continent.

Everything would be different if I were allowed to ride Rosie, Emily told herself as she marched across the yard. A gust of wind whipped her loose hair into wild disarray. Even the braid went flying. I'm ten now, she thought indignantly. Elizabeth Crowley will be competing at the county fair tomorrow, and she's two months younger than I am.

Emily's fists tightened when she thought how Elizabeth had showed off on her bay Morgan, jumping over bales of hay at the Crowley's barn raising last spring. I could beat Elizabeth if they'd let me ride Rosie, she said to herself. Now it was too late for this year's fair, but a fine time to start training for next year.

Pa had given Emily a hug and a sympathetic look when she had asked him. But he'd only said, "I'm sorry, Emmy. I promised Ma I wouldn't interfere. You'll have to talk to her yourself."

Emily sighed. It wouldn't be easy to convince Ma, she knew that. She had postponed asking her a long time, fearful that Ma would refuse. But she couldn't face Elizabeth at the fair tomorrow or watch the others competing in the races without at least having tried. Emily pushed open the door to the kitchen with one boot.

"I was about to send Tom for you," said her mother, glancing up from the butter churn. "Those pigs—" She stopped and stared at Emily. "What happened to your hair? Where's your bonnet?"

Emily reddened. What difference did it make if her hair wasn't neat? The pigs didn't care how she looked. She lifted a large iron pot off the back of the stove and poured its contents carefully into the slop pail. The kitchen was fragrant with the smell of stewing vegetables. "Ma?" Emily said. "There's something I want to ask you."

She took a step forward. "I don't see why I can't ride Rosie. You know I can ride as well as Tom."

"I've told you before, Emily, it isn't fitting for a lady

to ride at full gallop," Ma replied. "Rosie's young and high-spirited; she needs to gallop."

Emily's heart sank. She wanted to say that sometimes *she* needed to gallop, too, but she guessed what Ma would say to that.

"Besides, what if you fell, or got sick from overexertion? Galloping is too strenuous for you." Ever since Emily had almost died from scarlet fever as a baby, her mother had worried about her health. No amount of evidence to the contrary seemed to change Ma's perception of her as a frail child.

Emily hoisted the heavy pot to the sink and began to scour it with a brush, struggling to keep her voice steady. "I know I can handle Rosie, Ma. I've taken care of her since she was born. I know her better than— anyone. She's gentle and easy to manage. And Pa says that understanding a horse is more important than strength."

Emily ached at the unfairness of Tom riding Rosie while she had to plod along on Daisy or Mud, their plow horses. It made no difference if she kicked their sides and shouted "giddyap!" until December. I could go faster on a fence rail, she thought.

"Zeke says the girls out West ride as fast as the boys,"

Emily persisted. "He says a girl won all three riding competitions in Kansas last year."

"I won't have you growing up wild like those Kansas girls," Ma told her, churning steadily.

"Yes'm," said Emily. She thought she'd like to be wild, if it meant she could gallop Rosie. "Elizabeth Crowley will be riding her horse in the bareback races tomorrow," she added. Resentment cut through her like a March wind. "Other girls, too." Other girls whose mothers didn't hold to such notions, she thought. Emily had once heard Mrs. Crowley say that, when it came to healthful forms of exercise for young women, riding stood at the head of the list.

"Emily, I know it's disappointing for you. When I was your age, I wanted more than anything to go with my father on one of his surveying trips to the Southern states. But it meant traveling in a wagon in all kinds of weather through rough country, and I was needed at home to help care for my younger sisters."

Emily seized on her mother's softened tone. "If I rode Rosie," she pleaded, "I could go to town for you, or to Zeke's—I could be more help to you and Pa."

"When you are grown-up and responsible for your own welfare, that will be another matter," Ma told her.

"But while you are in my care, and we are so far from a doctor—" She went back to her churning. "I'm sorry, Em," she ended simply.

Discouraged, Emily picked up the slop pail and started for the door.

"Emily," her mother called when she was halfway down the porch steps. She felt a flicker of hope, but Ma only said, "Don't forget to finish your quilt block for the fair."

"Yes'm," said Emily, and tramped out to the pigpen. Clamoring pigs crowded toward her. A sow pushed her way to the front of the crowd and jammed her huge body against the heavy log enclosure, making it shake. "Stop it, Queen Victoria!" Emily said, pouring slops into the trough. She smiled as the sow, looking self-important and ridiculous, jostled the other pigs. "You're as bad as Tom," she said, and gave the sow a piece of potato that had stuck to the bottom of the pail.

On her way to the pasture Emily stopped at the root cellar for a handful of carrots. Rosie tossed her head and whinnied at her approach. She trotted over with high dancing steps, her rusty coat burnished by the sun.

"It's hopeless, Rosie," said Emily, feeding her and stroking the horse's soft, ruddy mane. Rosie chomped

noisily on the carrots. "No amount of reasoning will per-
suade Ma. I'll never get to ride you."

Rosie began to run around the pasture. As Emily
watched, she saw herself riding bareback around the
great open field at the fair, passing Elizabeth Crowley
to win by a length. The cheers of the crowd rang in her
ears.

When she headed back across the yard, her brothers
were standing at the edge of the chestnut grove, whis-
pering together.

"Hey, Em!" called Natty. He held a small canvas sack
in one hand.

Emily walked toward them. "Hey, yourself," she said
warily. "What's that?"

"We found a prince for you," said Tom. "Only you'll
have to free him from a spell. Show her, Natty."

Natty stuck his hand into the sack and thrust a large
toad in Emily's face. "Kiss it, *quick!*"

Emily grimaced and shoved her brother's arm away.
The toad squirmed from Natty's grip and bounded off.

"Should've kissed it while you had the chance," Tom
said, laughing.

"He's right," added Natty. "We ain't exactly on the

main route for princes." Natty and Tom collapsed, laughing, onto the ground.

Emily stormed past her brothers without a word and headed for the treehouse.

"It's—a shame," Natty spluttered. "Toad that big would've made a first-rate prince."

Tom stood up and pulled Natty with him. "C'mon," he said. "I've got to collect eggs." The boys headed off. Emily could hear their voices fading as she walked through the grove.

She drew her sewing basket from the hollow of the chestnut stump and climbed the ladder to the treehouse. Nothing would disturb her here, she thought. She worked the tangles out of her hair and braided it again. A wood thrush piped briefly; soft air blew around her face.

She set to work embroidering the letter P beside a large cloth pumpkin sewn to a square of fabric. *Ain't exactly on the main route for princes.* Through the branches she caught glimpses of the narrow wagon road that led to the Whilton Turnpike. A sparrow fluttered in the dirt, stirring up dust with its wings.

Emily thought back six weeks, when her family had traveled that road on the way to the Crowleys' barn raising. Elizabeth's brother Arthur had offered her a cup of lemonade. "It's a bit sour. We ran out of sugar," he had said, his eyes on the ground. She had not responded at first, thinking that he was talking to someone else. Her face burned again at the memory. After the new barn had been raised, Arthur had walked with her to the pasture and told her about the talents and peculiar habits of each of their horses. He must have been Tom's age— he was in Tom's grade at school—yet he had seemed interested in what she had to say, even respectful. It was both puzzling and pleasing.

Emily heard horse hooves coming down the road. As she listened, they grew slowly louder—a tedious, measured gait. Sure taking his time, she said to herself. Probably a visiting preacher. They always have old horses. She wrinkled her nose at the thought of the last such visitor, who had crowded her on the bench at dinner and smelled like tonic water. He had preached salvation until he grew hoarse, and her eyelids drooped.

But as the rider came into view, Emily saw bulging leather saddlebags, the telltale mark of a peddler. He wore a dark rumpled waistcoat and baggy striped trousers. His hat had a rounded crown and curved brim, upon which a layer of road dust had settled. She thought he had the boniest horse she'd ever seen, and immediately pitied the heavily laden animal. Emily was surprised when he dismounted and led the horse off the road in her direction. As they disappeared behind some trees, she wondered why he didn't ride up to the house, like most peddlers.

Curious, Emily inched forward until she caught a broken view of the peddler on the far side of an old oak. He tied his horse to a low branch and took off his hat. His head was bald—like a full moon, Emily thought.

The peddler opened a saddlebag and took out a silvery object which he placed somewhere in the branches before him. He wiped his face and neck with a cloth.

"The apple, the oak, and the weep-ing tree . . ." Singing to himself in a raspy bass, the peddler took something dark from the bag and laid it carefully on his head. A wig, Emily thought.

She shifted along the treehouse wall to keep the peddler in sight. " . . . *green grows the grass in Amer-i-kee. . . ."* He brushed the wig until it was as smooth as an otter's coat. Emily saw a flash of gold near his hand.

For a minute he seemed to be fidgeting with something just beneath his nose. Whatever it was made him sneeze so hard that his wig fell off. Emily laughed si-

lently into her hands. Was he taking snuff? Then the peddler turned and she saw his face. A fake moustache! What kind of peddler was this?

" *'Tis advertised in Boston, New York, and*—where the dickens!" he alternately sang and muttered as he rummaged in a pouch. "Ho, there! Stand still!" Emily caught glimpses of glittering objects before he took out something small and purplish and began to eat it. " *. . . and you'll all have fifty cents apiece, on the hundred and ninetieth da-ay . . .*" His horse tossed and whinnied hungrily, straining at the rope. The peddler reached in the bags again and threw something on the ground.

"Take it and be grateful, outcast from hell," he snapped. He yanked his ill-fitting waistcoat into place and peered in the direction of Emily's house.

She stared in surprise when the peddler drew out a large silver pitcher and tucked it under a strap near the saddle. Peddlers who had come to their farm in the past had sold tinware, shoes, items for a farmer's household. The peddlers themselves never owned anything of value.

He untied his swaybacked horse and led it toward the house. Emily watched uneasily, then scrambled down the ladder and ran after him. She could hear Tom and Natty calling out, greeting the peddler.

When she reached the house, he was already talking to her mother: " . . . all the way from Philadelphia, ma'am, supplying good folks like you with a powerful cleaning compound to destroy the villains dust, dirt, and tarnish which threaten your most cherished possessions."

"He should use a little on himself," whispered Natty to Tom.

Tom suppressed a smile.

The peddler shot a glance at the children, then turned back to their mother. With a dramatic flourish he pulled a small glass bottle from his waistcoat pocket. On the label were the words DR. FEVRIER'S MIRACLE CLEANER. "Named after the illustrious Professor Fevrier, whose reputation shines like"—he fumbled with the strap and produced the silver pitcher—"like this!" He turned it around. It was brilliantly shiny on one side, dull and pockmarked with stains on the other. "See for yourself what Dr. Fevrier's Miracle Cleaner can do."

"Just about *ruined* that side," Natty whispered to Tom, pointing to the tarnished half.

Tom started to laugh. At a warning look from Ma, he and Natty ran off.

Ma was examining the teapot. "Ma . . ." Emily began. Her cheeks burned. She had not considered what to say.

"What is it, Emily?" Ma's voice was strained.

The peddler stared at Emily with evident annoyance. Her eyes fell on his gaunt, drooping horse. Then she thought of something. There was one way to get Ma's immediate attention.

"I don't feel well," she said.

Her mother examined Emily's flushed face, then said to the peddler, "Won't you sit down, Mr.—?" She gestured toward a chair on the porch.

"Trout. Emanuel Trout." The peddler bowed. "I'll just see to my horse first," he said, patting its underfed flanks.

Ma directed him to hay and water. "I won't be a minute," she added.

"Ma, I'm sorry," said Emily as soon as they were in the house. "I lied to you. I feel fine."

Her mother looked at her in astonishment.

"I couldn't think how to get you away from the peddler," continued Emily. "And I had to warn you—"

"Warn me!" said Ma. "About what?"

"About him," said Emily, feeling somewhat confused. "He's not like other peddlers. He's wearing a wig and a false moustache. And he has lots of silver."

"How do you know all this?" Ma asked. "It isn't right to spy on people, no matter what you suspect."

"I wasn't spying. I was in the treehouse when he rode up. I couldn't help but see."

Her mother looked thoughtful. "You said he has silver?"

"There's the pitcher he showed you, plus a mirror— and his hairbrush shone like gold. It seemed like his saddlebags were clang-full of shiny things."

"The wig, hairbrush, and mirror speak more of vanity than villainy," Ma pointed out. "And the objects in his saddlebags might well have been tin pots. He displayed the pitcher without disguise. This hardly sounds like treachery."

Emily wondered why anyone would bother wearing a wig to peddle to farmers. But she only said, "He treats his horse cruelly but pretends kindness in front of us."

"His deception is so obvious that he can't pose any real danger," Ma told her. "He gives himself away too easily. But I'll promise you this, Emmy. I won't invite

him into the house, and I'll tell Pa your concerns when
he returns from the fields.

"You did right to tell me," Ma added as she started
to leave. "But while Mr. Trout is here, he is our guest
and your elder. I'll expect you to remember that."

"Yes'm," said Emily. She lingered in the kitchen after
Ma had gone. Ma was probably right, she told herself.
At any rate, Ma and Pa would keep an eye on Mr.
Trout. As she walked slowly toward the door, she heard
her mother's voice outside: " . . . little use for it, remote
as we are." Emily stopped to listen.

"Madam," said Mr. Trout, "you may be less remote
than you think. Why, last week I sold Dr. Fevrier's Miracle to twenty homesteaders' wives in Whilton County
alone."

For a minute their voices were too low to make out
the words; then Emily heard the peddler say, " . . .
building a Normal School down in Slippery Rock."

"You don't say!" Ma's voice held an eager interest.
"Slippery Rock is only an hour's ride on the Whilton
Turnpike. What else have you heard?"

"The Literary Society meets Wednesdays in Whisker-
ville . . ."

"Oh, my!" said Ma.

Oh, turnips! thought Emily as she headed back to the treehouse.

That night Emily awoke feeling uneasy. She had had a dream in which Mr. Trout was part of a band of outlaws. She lay in the dark room, thinking. The more she thought, the more uneasy she felt. Maybe the peddler was a scout. She'd heard about a gang of robbers who had terrorized towns in the Appalachian mountains last year and never been caught. A dozen lawless men could be gathering around her home right now, preparing for a raid.

Maybe preparing to steal horses! A wave of panic swept over her. She jumped out of bed, pulled a dress over her nightgown, and hurried to the boys' room.

"Tom!" she whispered, shaking him. "Wake up!"

Tom grunted drowsily.

"Mr. Trout is fixing to rob us!"

"Who?" Tom kept his eyes shut.

"Trout! The peddler!"

"*Rob* us? That mealy old peddler?" Tom stretched his

arms and looked at his sister in disgust. "What's he going to take—apple pie?"

She resisted the urge to pound him. "We've got horses, and Grandma Barrett's silver."

"A horse thief wouldn't ride a half-dead mare." Tom snorted and rolled over.

"He would if he were traveling in disguise," said Emily. "I watched him put on that wig and moustache. And his bags were filled with silver."

"Silver?" Tom turned back.

Emily nodded.

"Suppose he does come," Tom said, sitting up. "What then? How are you going to stop him?"

"I'll keep watch from the treehouse, but I need you to help. You wait in the barn with Rosie saddled. If he heads there, I'll signal you, and you can lead the other two horses up the hill."

"That's good; they'll follow Rosie." Tom sounded wide-awake now. "But what if he goes for the silver?"

"I'll keep it with me. But I'll signal so you can wake Pa."

"What are the signals?"

"Owl for the horses, frog for the silver." Emily headed toward the door.

"Em!" whispered Tom, struggling into his overalls. She stopped.

"I hate to lose a night's sleep for nothing."

"Then stay in bed," she said, and slipped quietly downstairs to the dark parlor.

Huddled in the treehouse beside the bulky mass of a flour sack containing a silver tea set, two platters, and a bowl, Emily strained to see the place where Mr. Trout had tied his horse. Would he come alone or with a gang? If I could ride Rosie, she thought, I wouldn't need Tom. I'd tie this sack to the saddle and lead the horses uphill myself.

The night was still except for the whine of crickets and an occasional brief scurrying in the brush. The moon was nearly full. Emily thought it looked like a silver plate shining through the branches. She rubbed her arms and wished she had thought to bring a shawl.

To keep awake, she spelled as many words as she could from the letters of her name: *my, lie, mile, lime, lye* . . . She thought of nine words, not including *Emil* and *Eli*, which were proper names.

It became harder and harder to keep her eyes open. Every now and then a branch snapped, and she would start and peer into the darkness. Then the leaves would whisper, *sleep, sleep,* and her head would begin to drop.

Once when she had been awakened by a mouse scurrying over her legs, she decided to try counting aloud to five hundred. She had lost count and was about to begin again when she heard a rushing sound in the air above her.

Straight overhead, like an immense shadow on the stars, were the outstretched wings of a great blue heron. It was so close that she thought she could have touched its dangling legs. For one second its huge wings seemed about to enfold the treehouse and carry her off. She shrank back against the wall. After the heron passed, she scrambled to her feet. She could hear the sound of its wings growing fainter, far off in the woods. At last she sat down and rested her head on her knees.

When she opened her eyes, the stars were faint; a red streak showed in the east. Her clothes were damp with dew, and her neck was sore. Shivering and somewhat dizzy, she got up and clambered down the ladder.

In the barn she ran past Tom, asleep on a pile of straw. She nearly cried with relief when she saw Rosie in her stall. Rosie whinnied softly and nuzzled her dress while Emily rubbed the horse's neck. She smiled sadly.

"If I were a boy, Rosie, we'd have more fun to the square inch—"

Tom groaned and sat up abruptly. "What happened?" he said, looking around.

"Nothing," said Emily.

"Did Trout—"

Emily shook her head.

"He wasn't any robber. I should've known. I'm a blamed fool to listen to your notions." Tom stood and brushed straw off his clothes. "It won't happen again, I tell you."

"It wasn't my notions when you tried to kill a dragon in the treehouse," said Emily indignantly, "or raise widow Parker's ghost in the cemetery at the church social. How about when you took it into your head to live on nothing but wild plants?"

Tom started, then recovered himself, and said with dignity, "That was a long time ago." He turned and left the barn.

By the time Emily had fed the horses and returned the silver to the parlor, she felt flushed and her head ached. When she entered the kitchen, her parents were already up. Ma, in her town dress, was packing food in a basket. Pa stood by the table in his black frock coat, the remains of breakfast at his place. Emily dropped into a chair.

Pa set his mug on the table. "Here she is now," he said, smiling at Emily. "Tom says you were doing chores early, to help us get a good start." Emily stared blankly at him.

"Tom!" Pa called up the stairs. "Come help me with the wagon."

"The wagon!" said Emily. Then she remembered. The county fair! Nearly everyone in Whilton County would be there—including Arthur Crowley. Why did it have to be today? Her heroic rescue had failed for lack of a villain; Tom and Natty were bound to make much of that. And she felt as if she hadn't slept at all. She groaned and put her head down on her arms.

"Why, Emmy, what's wrong? You don't look well." Ma held her wrist to Emily's forehead. "You're feverish! I shouldn't leave you here alone, and unwell," she went on in a worried tone. "But Pa's one of the judges, he *has* to go, and the horses are counted on for hauling, and I've promised the Ladies' Auxiliary . . ."

As her mother spoke, Emily had a brief vision of past fairs—rowing contests, jugglers, the three-legged race, which she and Tom had won two years in a row—and she almost convinced herself that she was well enough to go. But she didn't feel up to the long ride in a jostling wagon on the dusty road, or the heat and noise of the fair. She wanted only to lay her head on a cool pillow in her quiet room. For a brief moment, while her mother bent over her, she wished that Ma could stay, too. Then she remembered how Ma's constant, hovering care had broken into her rest when she'd been sick in the past.

"I just want to sleep," she said. "I'll be fine."

"I'll talk with your father," Ma said distractedly, heading to the door. "If he says—but I don't know, with you sick—"

Emily heard her parents talking outside. "It doesn't sound like much," said Pa, "and anyway, Emily can manage."

"We've never left her on her own before. Don't you think she needs—"

"What I think is that Emily is hardy, Georgina. Let her stay."

Finally Ma agreed. "Stay in bed, under the covers," Ma said. "Drink plenty of boneset tea. Keep the windows closed. And don't exert yourself."

The sun was rising as Emily watched her family leave

in the wagon. Daisy and Mud were hitched in front. Jars of Ma's preserves were packed carefully into boxes lined with straw. Nathaniel, squirming uncomfortably in his best clothes, sat wedged between Ma and Pa. Tom rode ahead on Rosie—the Napoleon of Whilton County, thought Emily. They would not be home until long after dark.

In the early afternoon, Emily awoke feeling more tired than before. It's hot as an oven in here, she thought. She lay for a while listening to the silence, and started at a sudden noise in the tree outside. What's the matter with you? she said to herself. It's nothing but a cicada. But she couldn't get rid of a sense of uneasiness.

She grabbed an old quilt and some apples. Under Tom's bed, she found an issue of *Young Folks* magazine, featuring the latest installment of *The Sea Cook, or Treasure Island*. She carried these to the treehouse, where she stretched herself out on the quilt. She could smell the heat, which rose in waves from the ground. Even in the shade, her head was burning. It was like lying too close to the fire. A pulsing chorus of insects thrummed around her. She tried to read, but her eyes ached. After a while she fell into a restless sleep.

In the middle of a dream in which Trout was drinking from a silver tumbler and singing in a grating, tuneless voice, she rolled over and opened her eyes. The voice from her dream continued, low and indistinct, but unmistakably real.

" . . . *blow you winds hi-ho, we'll clear a-way*—damn your hide, Lightning, *down!*" There was a loud crack, followed by a horse's frightened whinny.

On the wagon road, but much closer to the treehouse than he'd been the day before, Emanuel Trout sat on a tall black horse. Beside him stood a riderless horse that the peddler was leading by its reins. Both horses carried enormous saddlebags and shone with sweat. They paced constantly, sidestepping and tossing their heads. The sun beat down; the glare was blinding. Emily froze, afraid of making the slightest sound.

"*Clear a-way the running decks*—" Trout sang, then he coughed and spat onto the ground. His horse reared and whinnied loudly. Trout snapped the reins over its head. "Settle *down,* I said!" The other horse, a dappled grey with a black mane and tail, edged away nervously.

Emily held her breath, filled with a heavy dread.

"Monkey Pete should've done this house; it's *his* territory," Trout grumbled, taking a swig from a canteen strapped in front of his saddle. "But I had to go and tell him the road's a bone-buster." He took another drink, wiped his mouth with his hand. "Clod-headed, that's what I am," he muttered, and spat again. *"Blow you winds of the morn-in'—"*

Trout wiped his face on his sleeve and said, "I've a mind to burn down the shack of this mud-brained farmer and his no-mannered brats. What do you say to a little fire, Lightning?" He chuckled as he dismounted.

Tensing in anger and fear, Emily watched Trout tie the horses to a tree, remove the saddlebags from the grey horse, and start toward her house. Emily's thoughts raced. If she stayed in the treehouse, Trout might leave without noticing her. But he'd take their silver, maybe burn their house. The whole forest could burn. He could rob half the farmhouses in the county. There'd be no one home today to stop him.

She looked again at the horses. Perhaps she could ride the grey one. But what if Trout caught her before she got away? She shuddered and fought a wave of nausea.

Her eyes fell on her uneaten apples. Trembling, she

stuffed them into the pocket of her apron, hurried down the ladder, and ran to the horses. The dappled grey turned and whinnied. The black lowered its great head.

Emily held out the apples and glanced over her shoulder at the house. "Easy, now," she whispered, as much to herself as to the horses. The grey took the apple from her hand, but the black started and backed off.

Her hands shook as she untied both sets of reins and hauled herself up onto the saddle of the grey. She turned the horse toward the wagon road and dug her heels into its sides.

It bolted and tore down the road at a furious gallop. The black horse took off instantly and raced alongside. Unable to get her feet into the stirrups, Emily held tight to the saddle horn, bouncing painfully with every stride.

They galloped down the road between the woods and her family's fields. She tried not to look at the ground, dizzyingly far below, but her heart pounded every time the grey went over a ditch or swerved to avoid a branch. Whenever she ducked under a limb, the saddle horn jabbed her in the stomach.

Could Trout be following? Maybe he had another horse. What about the man he called Monkey Pete? She told herself that no one could catch her now, but she couldn't shake the sense that she was being followed.

Her heart dropped into her stomach when she saw the black horse pull up beside her and take the lead. Emily yanked hard on its reins, hauling back with her whole body, but that only seemed to make the black go faster. The dappled grey surged beneath her and tried to catch up. The horses raced down the uneven road at a terrifying speed. "Whoa, now, whoa," she called, pulling more gently this time. For a minute the grey regained the lead, but soon the black pulled away again. She could see its great neck stretching out. Within seconds it would be so far ahead that it would drag her off her horse.

She dropped the black's reins. For a minute longer it galloped ahead on the road, then suddenly swerved onto a path through Zeke's cornfield. As soon as the black was out of sight, Emily began to fear that it would return to Trout. Maybe Trout couldn't catch up with her, but she didn't want him to escape, either. For a few seconds she heard the black's hoofbeats; then the sound faded and was lost.

She passed Zeke's fields and the road that led to his

house. If only Zeke were home, she thought, but he'd be at the fair like everyone else.

The crossroads lay just ahead, with the smoothly graded dirt of the Whilton Turnpike stretching far in both directions. The familiar crossroads sign was near enough to read, but Emily didn't need to; she had traveled this road since she was four. She steered the grey horse to the left; it wheeled and galloped down the turnpike.

As they turned, Emily looked back down the wagon road. There was no sign of the black horse.

After a long field of buckwheat, they passed a brick farmhouse half-hidden by an apple orchard. I should have seen the school by now, she thought. They crossed a wooden bridge; she caught a quick glimpse of boulders in a stream before they came to a pasture and a barn with a blue roof. None of this looked familiar. Where was the school? She began to think she had turned in the wrong direction. Then she recognized a stone house on her right. She must have passed the school without noticing.

The horse was still galloping rapidly. Emily felt as if she was burning up; her head throbbed painfully, and

sweat fell into her eyes. I've got to slow it down, she thought. She tugged hard, but the grey set its head and pulled back on her hands.

"Easy, now, don't be frightened," she said. "No one's going to hurt you."

She continued talking in a soothing voice, easing gently on the reins. They passed a church and another farm before the road descended into a heavily wooded valley. Finally the grey slowed into a smooth, graceful canter. Emily felt as if the ground had dropped away and she were flying. Although she still tensed forward, fearful that the horse would bolt, she couldn't help but smile. *This* is what she had dreamed of every time she had groomed Rosie or watched her run.

When they crossed the Little Moraine River, Emily caught a glimpse of the buildings of Brewster's Mill on the far horizon. It would not be long now until the fairgrounds.

She thought about what she would do when she got there. Sheriff Perly would most likely be found near the exhibition tents or at the great field where horse races and award ceremonies were held. She'd look for him first, then find Ma and Pa.

It seemed like only moments later when she began to

see wagons parked along the road. The racing field was just past the next bend. Emily began to worry about what the grey might do when it saw crowds of people.

Before she could give it any thought, she rounded the bend and found herself at one end of the open field. Huge crowds thronged both sides, while at the far end several horses with riders stood before the judges' platform. Emily turned the grey toward the platform.

A murmur rose in the crowd as she rode across the field. The grey whinnied. "Steady, now, almost there," she said, and kept a firm hold on the reins. The horses in front of the platform paced nervously. Arthur was among the riders.

She brought the grey to a stop at the platform and dismounted quickly. Her legs wobbled, and she stumbled as she led the horse forward. "Sheriff Perly—" she began.

Just then there was a long whinny and the sound of approaching hooves. Shouts rose as the black horse, riderless, entered the field and trotted swiftly toward her. For a frightening moment she thought it would run past her into the crowd, but it stopped suddenly, right beside the grey.

Emily grabbed the black's reins and led both horses

to the platform, where the sheriff stood frozen in amazement.

"I've come to report a robber," said Emily.

———

That evening, five Whilton County farmers restored silver and jewelry to places of safekeeping. Emanuel Trout and Monkey Pete dined on weak tea and stale bread in all the elegance and comfort of the Brewster's Mill jail.

Emily rested in bed, a mustard plaster on her chest. She had ridden home in the wagon with her family. On the way, Tom and Natty had pestered her for details: which tree Trout had tied his horses to, whether he'd carried a gun, and the words to the songs he'd sung, until Pa had told them to leave her in peace.

"Well, Georgina," she'd heard him say to Ma, "it seems Emily can already handle herself on a horse. All she needs is practice."

Ma had only said, "After she's well, then we'll see." Remembering Ma's words, Emily wanted to leap in the air and shout. It wasn't quite a promise, but it was a good sign.

Emily lay awake for a long time, thinking. How strange that it was Trout who had given her a horse to gallop. She smiled. Maybe she should have kissed Natty's toad, after all. *Ain't exactly on the main route for princes.*

The moon rose above the trees and spilled light into her room. Emily yawned and stretched her legs beneath the covers. She let her eyes close. Deep in the woods a frog grumbled. Somewhere, she felt sure, a heron was flying.

That Story about the Cherry Tree

March
1 8 8 4

Natty glanced again at the clock on Miss Aderley's desk. One-fifteen. Only two more hours until school let out. He sank lower on the bench and looked outside. He thought about Pa, who was in Brewster's Mill with Tom right now, buying sheep. Natty harbored no tender feelings for these sheep. They weren't even home yet, and already they were making him miserable.

If only he'd spoken to Pa at breakfast, maybe he could have stopped him. But there hadn't been much chance. Pa had announced his intention of buying sheep several weeks earlier, but only that morning had he mentioned they were to be Natty's.

The way Pa saw it, they were to be the start of a large and prosperous ranch that Natty would manage when he grew up. "Pure merinos, Natty! We'll be among the first in Whilton County to raise this breed," Pa had said. "Their wool is worth its weight in gold in Philadelphia. If you start now you'll have a good flock by the time you finish school." At first Natty had been too surprised to speak, or even think clearly. Then Ma had called him to bring firewood, and Pa had set off for town before Natty could respond.

It wasn't that Natty had anything against sheep. He had watched a sheep-shearing demonstration at the county fair last summer, but he had never given sheep much thought until today.

Nor had he thought much about what he would do once he grew up. Pa seemed to have it all worked out: Tom would manage the field crops, and Natty would raise sheep.

He tried to picture himself holding down an enormous ram like the man at the fair. He remembered the ram's powerful horns and hooves: six reasons not to get close to a ram, he had said to himself. Still, he wouldn't have minded taking care of some sheep if it weren't for the sense that they were about to take care of him, for good. Natty sighed. It was too late to stop Pa from buying the sheep.

The trees outside the schoolhouse were dark and shiny from the rain. A gust of wind spattered water off the branches. Suddenly Natty sat up straight, and his face brightened. Maybe he could convince Pa to think of the sheep as only another chore, a job that would pass out of Natty's hands when he grew up and left home. After all, Natty had been cleaning the hen house and chopping kindling for over a year, and no one had ever suggested that he might start a poultry business or become a lumberjack.

"Nathaniel Barrett, this is the third time today I have found you dreaming." Miss Aderley knelt beside the desk and looked at him earnestly. She frowned, but there was something in her dark eyes and gentle voice which reassured him. "I don't want to have to ask you to remain after school."

"Yes, Miss Aderley," said Natty. He turned away from the window.

Miss Aderley straightened and called the class to attention. "Today we are going to hear a famous story. It will give us a portrait of our first president as a youth. I will ask each of the students in grades two through four to read aloud in turn. Please open your readers to page forty-eight, *'George Washington and the Cherry Tree.'*"

Miss Aderley always had them read in order of age, oldest first. Natty glanced at Celia Chandler, who sat on his right. The only other seven-year-old in the school, she would read just before him. His gaze fell on the book they shared, but his thoughts were elsewhere. What if he came up with his own plan? he wondered. Would Pa give up on the sheep ranch?

Behind him, a high-pitched voice declaimed: "*. . . the oldest of five children by his second wife. In 1732, the family moved to a plantation . . .*"

Celia's father was a banker in town. Natty thought about the gold letters on the bank window, the smell of leather, the low chime of Mr. Chandler's grandfather clock. Maybe he'd be a banker.

At the other end of his row, nine-year-old Corbett Gray was reading: "*. . . and brought the little sapling all the way from . . .*"

Or he could be a judge. The three-story stone courthouse was the tallest building in Brewster's Mill. There had been a parade to celebrate its opening. His pulse quickening, he thought back to the capture of Emanuel

Trout this past summer. Everyone looked up to Judge Shanks and Sheriff Perly. But they seemed to look up to Mr. Chandler even more.

As one by one the others in his row stood to take their turns, Natty considered what it would be like to be a doctor, a store owner, or a cowboy.

Then Celia rose beside him. *"On the Chesapeake plantations the principal crops were corn . . ."* she began, joining words together in a breathless jumble. Natty listened without enthusiasm as Celia described Mr. Washington's crops, how tall George grew, and how the cherry tree grew even taller, until the story took a turn which nearly jolted him out of his seat.

George Washington chopped down his father's cherry tree! Why would he do a thing like that? Pa would tan his hide if— He looked up with sudden interest as Celia continued: *" 'Did you cut down my cherry tree?' demanded Mr. Washington. 'Father, I cannot tell a lie,' replied George. 'It was I who cut down your tree.' "*

George turned himself in! thought Natty. What would Mr. Washington—

"Nathaniel Barrett!" Miss Aderley called from her desk. He looked up. He hadn't noticed Celia stop reading. "It's your turn, Nathaniel," prompted Miss Aderley.

He stood and read: *"Mr. Washington, impressed by his son's honesty and courage, knew that George was destined for greatness. From that day forward he gave George every opportunity to develop his considerable talents. By the age of ten, George was the best horseman in Virginia, with two horses of his own. He dreamed of being a soldier, ship's captain, or explorer. Mr. Washington left his son free to follow a path of his own choosing."* Natty looked at his teacher, his eyes wide.

"You read with feeling, Nathaniel," said Miss Aderley, smiling her approval. She turned to write a list of spelling words on the board.

Natty dropped back on the bench and looked out the window as if reassuring himself that everything was still there, trees on the ground and clouds in the sky, and not the other way around. He could hardly believe what he had just read: George Washington confessed to cutting down his father's prize cherry tree—for no reason at all—and his father didn't punish him. Instead he rewarded George! Nathaniel stared at the words once again: *A path of his own choosing.* These words had been written for him!

He let out a long breath and relaxed for the first time since breakfast. The story had given him the way to get through to Pa. He'd do what George had done. Miss Aderley had said that the story of the cherry tree was famous; Pa was sure to know it.

The rain had stopped when Natty sloshed along the leaf-covered road to his home. Deep in the woods, patches of snow still fringed the tree trunks like lace collars. The air was fresh and cool, smelling of mud. Water dripped steadily off the tips of branches. It reminded Natty of summer, the way water ran off his arms and hands when he climbed out of the pond.

He walked alone. Most days he would have ridden behind Emily on Rosie, but today Emily had stayed home to help Ma make preserves. Natty didn't mind; it gave him time to think about what he had to do. The more he thought about it, the more he felt sure that it would work.

He pictured himself standing in the yard, axe in hand, beside a fallen cherry tree. Pa would see him and— Natty stopped. They didn't have a cherry tree on their farm. He brushed aside this problem. He'd work out the details later.

The main thing was, Pa would let Natty make his own plans from now on. He could take his time, make choices, as George had done. He felt a rush of excitement. Maybe he'd even get to be president of the United States!

Natty smiled as he entered the quiet farmyard. Pa and Tom would not be back from Brewster's Mill until supper. Emily and Ma were busy in the kitchen. Since Natty often did chores before entering the house, Ma would not miss him for a while.

First, I have to find the right tree, he thought. He placed his books on the top step of the porch.

Two apple trees stood nearby, a few withered leaves drooping from their branches. They were the closest thing to a cherry tree on the farm. Natty envisioned a slice of his mother's high-crusted apple pie, covered with cinnamon and cream, and decided to see what he could find in the chestnut grove.

As he walked past the chicken coop and into the woods, he watched a squirrel dig up an acorn, scurry a few yards, and start to bury it again. The oaks were so big he couldn't reach around their trunks. He would need to find something much smaller if he were to cut it down before Pa came home. And it had to be special, a tree which stood out from the others. He sighed. Finding the right tree wasn't going to be easy.

The sun was low in the sky. Natty shuffled through

a thick mat of wet leaves and climbed into the treehouse. He ducked so as not to jostle the branches above him, the first stage of a roof which he and Tom had started to build last fall. Although they had intended to reinforce the branches and then cover them with shingles, they'd never gotten around to it.

Natty gazed at a small clearing near the treehouse. In the center of the clearing rose the only maple tree in their woods. Pa had said the maple seed must have blown over from a neighboring homestead. It had grown quickly in its patch of sunlight and was now twice the height of the treehouse. The slanting rays of the sun struck three dark red leaves trembling at the top—like feathers on a lady's hat, Natty thought. A smile spread across his face. That's the tree! he said to himself.

Natty clambered down and ran to the barn, where Pa's tools hung on a wall. He struggled to lift the axe, then set it back in place. George Washington must have been a strong kid, he thought. He paused a moment. He wanted to follow the story exactly, so that everything would turn out as it should. Yet here he was without a cherry tree and unable to lift an axe.

Would a hatchet do? A hatchet *was* an axe, when you

thought about it; he had even heard it called a "hand axe." And the maple's trunk was thin; he'd chopped kindling almost that big with a hatchet.

He returned to the maple tree and took a swing at the trunk. The hatchet nicked the ruddy bark and slid into the soil. He swung again, missing completely. Then the blade went straight into the trunk and stuck there.

Natty stopped, panting. Cutting down an upright tree was a lot harder than splitting pieces of kindling on a chopping block. He wiggled out the blade and tried again, and at last succeeded in chopping a wedge in the trunk. The sun had turned deep red, and daylight was fading in the woods. His chest tightened. Pa'll be home soon, he thought.

Then he dropped the hatchet and stared, dejected, at the maple tree. Pa wouldn't even *see* this tree, way back here! He sighed. He *had* to cut it down, now that he'd gotten this far. He could drag it into the yard to show Pa. But working with the hatchet was too slow.

He returned the hatchet to the barn and got down a saw. Several teeth were missing. Just like me, thought Natty, grinning.

Back at the maple tree, he placed the jagged blade in the center of the wedge. He pulled the saw toward him;

it cut a straight line in the wood. Natty glanced at the top branches. A chill went through him. *Don't fall on me,* he begged silently.

Natty dragged the heavy saw back and forth, back and forth, grunting with the effort. The blade dug into the wood, shaking the branches. He labored on; the saw rasped and the tree creaked. The sound of Pa's wagon startled him. Natty looked up. The tree leaned precariously over the treehouse.

"No!" he shouted in alarm. "No! The other way!" He backed off, panting, motioning frantically to the tree.

As he stared in horror, the tree tottered, and with one long, sickening crack, smashed through the treehouse roof and one wall, and shuddered to rest. In a matter of seconds the treehouse was gone. In its place was a gigantic tangle of branches. It looked like the crazy nest of some enormous bird. Natty suddenly remembered a newspaper story his father had read to him about a house blown into a tree by a tornado. But this was no tornado; he had done this himself. A red leaf floated to the ground by his feet. Tom and Emmy'll *never* forgive me, he thought. He sank to his knees and gazed at the ruins.

"Natty! *Nat-ty!*" came Pa's voice from the yard. Natty

started, remembering the sheep. His plan seemed to have splintered like the treehouse. He stood up, swallowing against a lump in his throat. There was no way to drag the tree to the farmyard now, and no time to cut another. He'd have to bring his father to the tree.

Fighting a rising sense of defeat, he hurried to the barn. He ran past the wagon standing empty in the middle of the darkening yard. Where were the sheep? He hesitated a moment at the barn door, then stepped inside.

His father was sitting in an open pen with something on his lap. At first it looked to Natty like a bundle of grey blanket. On the ground beside him was another bundle, stirring slightly and making small, thin sounds. Pa looked up and smiled. He held a glass bottle with a rubber nipple in one hand and was feeding the lamb on his lap.

The lamb's head and hooves were black; the rest of its tiny body was covered with curly beige wool. Something caught in Natty's throat at the sight of its delicate head stretching out toward the milk.

"They still need milk for a few more weeks," Pa told him. "Would you like to feed them? They're yours, you know."

Watching the tiny lambs, Natty ached to hold one and feed it from the bottle. As he became aware of this, prickles of alarm rose at the back of his neck. He struggled to focus on George Washington, the tree, and what he still had to do. It wasn't fair, he thought. He had a feeling things might have gone differently for George if he had had to watch lambs drinking from a bottle before he headed out with that axe.

The lamb finished the milk and continued to suck noisily, drawing air. Pa gently released its mouth from the nipple.

Natty didn't think he could hold out much longer. The prickles spread across his shoulders and down his back. What would he do if Pa walked over and actually put a lamb into his arms?

He shoved his hands into his overalls. "Pa," he said. "There—there's something I have to show you. Something important."

Pa looked at him, puzzled. "All right, Natty. After I finish feeding this one."

Natty tried to focus on the space on the wall where the saw usually hung, but found his eyes drawn back to the lambs. The lamb that had drunk first rose on its thin legs and nibbled at Pa's sleeve.

Then, as Pa stood up and Natty was turning away with a mixture of relief and regret, one of the lambs bounded from the pen toward the open barn door. It didn't run or walk; it bounced as if its legs were on springs.

Natty was so surprised that he made no move to catch it. His father had to dive after it to stop it from bouncing right out of the barn.

He watched without breathing as Pa carried the lamb back to the pen and closed it in. Natty had been unprepared for lambs that drank from bottles and bounced.

In silence he led Pa to the treehouse. Pa made a strange, choking noise as he stared at it. Natty clenched his hands; they were cold as ice. He looked anxiously at his father, hoping to hear the question made famous by another father, on a farm in Virginia, over a hundred years ago.

"Looks like you—ah—finished the roof," Pa said.

Natty started, then shook his head in disbelief. The school reader clearly said that *every generation* since George Washington knew the story of the cherry tree!

Maybe Pa needed some prompting. "Father, I cannot tell a lie—" he began.

Pa raised his eyebrows. A smile played at the corners of his mouth.

Natty tried to steady his voice. "It was I who cut down the tree. *And* broke the treehouse roof," he added, his voice cracking. Why didn't Pa get it? When would he act like he was supposed to? Natty shifted uneasily under his father's gaze.

Pa walked to the fallen maple and examined the trunk. He glanced at the mess on top of the treehouse. "Why?" he said.

Natty felt a pang of despair. Being brave and telling the truth only counts if your father notices it, he thought. "Because I"—his voice dropped—"I want to be president of the United States when I grow up."

Pa stared at him in surprise.

"I didn't mean to wreck the treehouse," said Natty, giving way to tears of disappointment and shame. "I only meant to cut down the tree, but it—it took a path of its own choosing."

There must be more to that story about the cherry tree, he thought.

Natty sat in the dark barn, two lambs on his lap. They had just finished a bottle of milk and were asleep. A lantern on the opposite wall cast a pale yellow circle onto the ground. I ought to be asleep, too, thought Natty. He had promised Pa he wouldn't stay long. But he couldn't leave, not yet.

It can't hurt to keep an eye on them, he told himself. A lamb could bounce its way into all kinds of trouble. But he knew that wasn't why he had raced through his chores and dinner to come out here.

He let out a long breath and leaned back against the wall. He had always loved the barn at night: the smell of hay and animals, the sound of chewing, an occasional whicker from a horse, and scuttling in the hayloft. Bats flew in crooked paths in and out of the half-open door. He had never thought anything missing, before. But he would never again think a barn complete unless it had lambs.

A lamb stirred in its sleep. Natty stroked the tight fuzzy curls on its back. "My pa isn't much like George Washington's father," he whispered.

No, he thought, not at all like Mr. Washington. Their conversation at the treehouse had been perhaps the

most surprising event of the day. Pa had readily agreed to Natty's offer to care for the lambs on a trial basis, with nothing settled for the future. Nothing except that Natty, like George Washington, would choose his own course. And he'd also repair the treehouse, starting tomorrow.

Natty yawned and set the lambs on a pile of straw. He took the lantern and went out, closing the gate behind him.

The yard looked silvery under a half moon. Maybe, he thought, he'd have a sheep ranch *and* become president. Why not? Even though a person was destined for greatness, he could also be destined to love lambs. Suddenly Natty wanted to bounce across the farmyard like the lambs. He raced to the house and up the steps.

Anne Isaacs lives in Santa Cruz, California, where her husband and children built their own treehouse. She received a *Publishers Weekly* Cuffie Award for "Most Promising New Author" for her first book, *Swamp Angel*, a Caldecott Honor Book illustrated by Paul O. Zelinsky.

Lloyd Bloom is an award-winning painter and illustrator. He illustrated the Newbery Honor Book *Like Jake and Me*, by Mavis Jukes, and the award-winning *Yonder,* by Tony Johnston. He lives in Brooklyn, New York.

OTHER PUFFIN BOOKS YOU MAY ENJOY

The Bears' House   Marilyn Sachs

Bound for Oregon   Jean Van Leeuwen

A Gift for Mama   Hautzig/Diamond

Hide and Seek   Ida Vos

The House on Walenska Street   Herman/Avishai

Red-Dirt Jessie   Anna Myers

Sasha and the Wolfcub   Jungman/Wright

Spiderweb for Two   Elizabeth Enright

Spotting the Leopard   Anna Myers

Then There Were Five   Elizabeth Enright